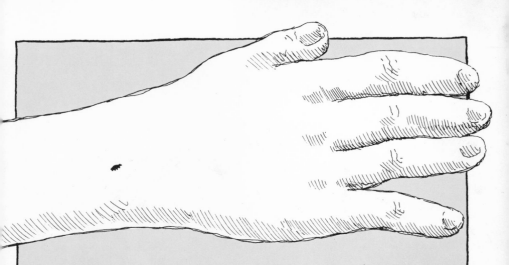

FIONA'S FLEA

FIONA'S FLEA

by Beverly Keller

pictures by Diane Paterson

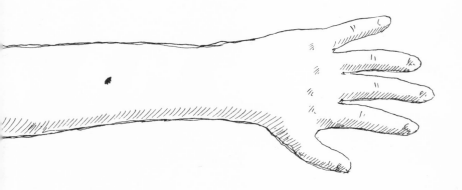

Coward, McCann & Geoghegan, Inc.   New York

26395

LIBRARY OF CONGRESS CATALOGING IN PUBLICATION DATA

Keller, Beverly.
  Fiona's flea.
  (A Break-of-day book)
  SUMMARY: Fiona befriends a flea and helps get it
started in show business.
  [1. Fleas—fiction] I. Paterson, Diane,
1946-   II. Title.
PZ7.K2813Fi   [E]   80-16853
ISBN 0-698-30719-4

First printing
Printed in the United States of America

for Ferd Monjo

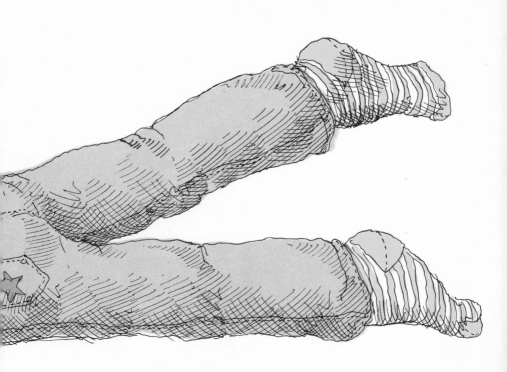

Fiona Foster lay on the floor
looking at the comics page
and worrying her parents.
"You can't mope around all day
and expect us to take you
to the circus tonight,"
her mother warned.
"And how would you feel
if you missed the circus?"

Fiona did not look up,
but she mumbled, "Glad."

"What did she say?"
her father asked.

"She said she'd feel bad,"
Fiona's mother told him.

"I thought she said *mad*."

Mrs. Foster frowned.
"Maybe she said *sad*."

Fiona looked up from the comics.
"I said glad."

"No, no," her father said.
"We're talking about how you'd feel
if you *missed* the circus."

"Glad," Fiona repeated.

"Fiona," Mrs. Foster said firmly,
"every child loves a circus."

"I don't," Fiona said.
She saw that they were shocked.
"Maybe I'd better go to the park now,
so you can talk about me
while I'm not around."

Barbara and Larry and Howard
were at the park.
Howard's dog Spike was on a leash.
Barbara's brother Oliver
was in a stroller,
trying to chew Spike's leash.

"What are you going to wear
to the circus?" Barbara asked Fiona.

"I'm not going," Fiona said.

Larry looked at her with respect.
"You must have done something awful
to be kept home from the circus!"

"I don't want to go,"
Fiona confessed.

Larry was amazed.
"You mean you don't want to see
all the lions and tigers?"

Fiona watched a bug
wander across the path.
"Lions and tigers
do not belong in cages."

Barbara looked worried.
"But what about the elephants?
You'll miss all the elephants."

"With chains on their legs?"
Fiona watched Spike
roll in the grass.
"Elephants put up with too much."

"Okay. Forget elephants,"
Barbara said.
"How about the clowns?
You can't have anything against clowns."

Fiona shivered.
"They have scary faces
and their shoes make me nervous."

"You just want to ruin everything
for everybody, Fiona Foster!"
Barbara jumped up
and wheeled Oliver away.
Larry and Howard left with Spike.
Fiona went home.

She filled her dog dish with water
and put it on the porch,
in case some dog
dropped by for a drink.
Then she sat on the porch steps
eating old grapes.

A skinny, shivery stray dog
wandered near.
"Have a drink," Fiona offered.

He scrunched down on the sidewalk
and waited for her
to throw something at him.
A stray dog,
and not very handsome,
he was used to being yelled at
and chased.
He knew it was no use to run.
Things people threw
went faster than he could.

"Have a grape," Fiona urged.

Dogs do not eat grapes.
But this dog had gone a long time
with nothing to eat.
A grape was something.
He crept a little closer.
Nervously, he nibbled a grape.
Then he ate the bunch.
He drank the water
and stepped in the dog dish.
Finally he sat on the step
and leaned against Fiona.

Her parents came out.
"Get that flea-bitten dog
off our porch," her father ordered.

The dog scrambled off the step
and around the corner.

"You didn't have to insult him!"
Fiona cried.

"He was covered with fleas,"
her mother said.

Fiona ran after the stray.
When she found him,
he scrunched down, shivering.
After she had petted him awhile,
he followed her to the park
and sat watching her think.
When Fiona saw her friends coming,
she put her arm around him
so he wouldn't run again.

"That's the worst-looking
old flea-bitten dog I ever saw,"
Larry declared.

"He'd better not get fleas
all over Spike," Howard warned.

Barbara held Oliver back.
"I don't want any fleas on my brother.
He'd eat them."

Fiona hugged the stray.

"You're going to get fleas,"
Larry told her.

"Look! Look! Look!"
Barbara pointed.
"She's got one!"

A tiny flea had settled
on Fiona's wrist.

"Squash it before it bites,"
Barbara urged.

Fiona peered at the flea,
which was barely big enough to see.
"Oliver bites,
and nobody squashes him."

"He's too big," Barbara said.

Howard glowered at the flea.
"Shake it off on the grass."

Fiona hesitated.
"Do fleas live on grass?"

"They die on grass," Larry said.
"They only live on animals
—or people."

Fiona looked down at the flea.
She pictured that poor speck
lost in a grass jungle,
dying alone,
with nobody to hold
its flea hand—or foot.

"Why don't you put it
back on the dog?" Barbara suggested.

Fiona gazed at the stray.
"Don't fleas bite dogs?"

"Sure. And dogs scratch fleas,"
Larry said.

The flea was hardly more than a dot,
and the dog's claws were long and thick.
"That could be hard on the flea."
Fiona felt a tiny sharp itch
on her wrist.
"I think it bit me."

Barbara grabbed Oliver's stroller.
"I don't want my brother
near a person who has fleas!"

"Take Spike with you, Barbara,"
Howard said.
"I'm not having my dog
around any flea-bitten person."

Fiona closed her eyes
and wished she were anybody else
—even Oliver—even a *clown*.

"Listen, Fiona," Howard said,
"you can't keep that flea on you.
How will you feel when word gets around?
How will you feel when it's written
on all the sidewalks—
Fiona Foster wears fleas?"

Fiona clapped her flea-free hand
over her ear.

"There's no place you can go
with a flea all over you—
except maybe a flea circus,"
he went on.

Fiona took her hand off her ear.
"Flea circus?"

"They used to have them
in the old days," Larry said.
"There were fleas in little tents
doing tricks."

Fiona opened her eyes.
"You mean people tamed these tiny things
with whips?"

"Come *on*." Howard snorted.
"A whip would wipe out the whole circus."

"This was more of a show than a circus,"
Larry said.
"A flea show was probably
the only place in the world
where a flea wouldn't
be sprayed or squashed or scratched."

Fiona felt another small nip
on her wrist.
"I don't suppose they still have
flea shows anymore."

"There's a flea market
down by the bus station,"
Howard reminded her.

"Sometimes you are really dumb,"
Larry scoffed.
"They sell old furniture and junk
at flea markets.
Nobody sells *fleas*."

Fiona scratched, carefully.
"It wouldn't hurt
just to walk down there."

Larry went home.
The stray dog followed Howard and Fiona
to the flea market.

"You talk while I stay back,"
Fiona told Howard.
"I don't know how people would feel
having a real flea around."

Howard found an old man
near a stall full of crooked lamps
and broken toasters.
"Um . . . I'm wondering about fleas."

The man looked down at him.
"You want to buy a *flea*?"

"I just wanted to know
about a flea circus."

The man smiled.
"Son, there hasn't been
a flea circus in this town
in years."

Howard and Fiona and the dog
were scuffing across the road
when they heard behind them,
"FLEA CIRCUS!"
The old man caught up with them.
"What an idea!
I've been running that flea market
for years and I never thought of it.
Imagine—the first flea market
in the world
to have a grand and glorious,
old-time, genuine American *flea circus!*
But what am I talking about?
You can't find a flea circus
in this day and age.
You can't even find a flea
with any manners."
He trudged back toward his flea market.

"I didn't mean to ruin his day."
Howard looked at the flea bites
on Fiona's arm.
"There's one last chance.
Maybe an animal trainer
would know how fleas
used to be tamed."

"You mean a trainer
from the big circus?"

"Look, Fiona.
There could be some nice way
to teach a flea not to bite."

An old woman
who was poking through a trash can
looked up. "You're not going to find
anybody who trains fleas anymore.
The last person I knew who trained fleas
was my daddy,
when we had our flea show."

"Was it like a flea circus?"
Fiona asked.

"Never!
We didn't coop up our fleas
in a cage, like animals."

"I suppose they'd just walk out
between the bars," Howard said.

The old woman nodded.
"Besides, if you don't treat a flea
just right,
he'll die on you."

"*On* you?" Fiona glanced at her arm.

"Oh, a flea doesn't ask for much,
just a cozy space,
a little nip from a friendly person.
But why am I going on like this?
Nobody cares about fleas anymore."

"The man who runs the flea market does,"
Fiona said. "He wants a flea circus."

The woman grabbed her arm. "He does?"

"Look out!" Fiona cried. "My flea!"

The woman let go
and peered at the flea.
"He's all right. Poor dear!
How could anyone hurt a flea?
But tell me about this man."

Fiona did.

"You don't suppose he'd settle
for a flea *show?*"
the woman asked.

"I sure would," Howard said.

"Just let me tidy up."
The woman ran a piece of comb
through her hair.
"I know I could put together
a great show.
After all, I grew up with fleas!"

They found the man
near a table of old books.

"We brought you a famous flea trainer!"
Howard announced.

The woman brushed dust off her skirt.
"My name is Mardella Wax.
I may not look like much,
but, believe me, I know fleas."

"I could tell that
the minute I set eyes on you."
Taking them to a rickety stall,
the man bought them all
greasy doughnuts.

He and Mardella talked fleas
and business,
and finally shook hands.
He gave Howard and Fiona
a bag of sticky taffy,
fed the stray another doughnut,
and said, "See you Saturday,"
to Mardella Wax.

"Just one more thing," Mardella said.
"After this, my dog eats
no more greasy doughnuts."

The man looked surprised.
"Your dog?"

"From now on he is.

You can see he needs a person."
She knelt beside the stray
and parted his fur.
"Look at those fleas.
All that talent, just trying to get by
in the dust and dirt.
Once I've coaxed them off him,
I'll give him a bath
and some proper food.
He'll sit outside my ticket booth
and call people over.
Every good show needs a barker."

"How will you keep the fleas
off him?" Fiona asked.

Mardella Wax patted the stray
very carefully.
"In a week, these fleas
wouldn't be caught dead on a dog.
You'll see.
You'll be my special honored guests."

Fiona held out her arm.
"What about this one?"

Mardella Wax looked closely
at Fiona's flea. "This one?
Anybody with half an eye
could see that *this* one
was born to be a star.
Come along, you little nipper."

Howard watched her leave,
the flea on her hand,
the dog following her.
"Do you think we did the right thing?"
he asked Fiona.

"I hope so," Fiona said,
"since it's the only thing
we could think of."

When she got home,
her parents were cross.
"You refuse to go to a circus,
you chase after stray dogs,
then you come home
scratching like a monkey
and carrying a bag of sticky taffy,"
her father stormed.

"Half a bag," she murmured.

"Get right in the tub,"
her mother ordered.

As Fiona lay back
scratching in a sea of bubbles,
her mother came into the bathroom.
"Good heavens!
Did you use all the bubble bath?"

"I deserve it."
Fiona stretched her toes.
"I saved a life,
and I got dozens more
into show business."

About the Author

BEVERLY KELLER was born in San Francisco and attended schools in Colorado, South Dakota, Nebraska, Washington, D.C., and California. A period spent living in the Middle East inspired her to write an espionage novel, *The Baghdad Defections.* Since then she has written five well-received children's books: *Fiona's Bee, Don't Throw Another One, Dover!, The Beetle Bush,* and *Pimm's Place,* all picture books; and for older readers: *The Genuine, Ingenious Thrift Shop Genie, Clarissa Mae Bean & Me.*

Ms. Keller makes her home in Davis, California.

About the Artist

DIANE PATERSON lives in High Falls, N.Y., with her two daughters, two cats, a chicken and a rooster, and a dozen turkeys. She has written and illustrated about twenty books so far, including *Fiona's Bee,* and is now working on a giant storybook for children.